Cheap Skates

George Shea

SPRINT BOOKS

SCHOLASTIC BOOK SERVICES
New York Toronto London Auckland Sydney Tokyo

For John MacLean

Cover and interior photography by Richard Hutchings
Cover illustration by Don Brautigan

This book is from Sprint Starter Library C.
Other books in this library are:
Space Scooter
Jody
The Shortest Sheriff in the West
Adventure at the Wax Museum

ISBN 0-590-30973-0
Copyright © 1980 by George Shea. All rights reserved. Published by Scholastic Book
Services, a division of Scholastic Magazines, Inc.

12 11 10 9 8 7 6 5 4 3 2 1   9   0 1 2 3 4 5/8

chapter 1

Joe was new on Broom Street. His family had just moved there. He missed his old friends a lot, but now he wanted to make new ones.

He looked across the street to the park. The kids who lived on his block played there. They

were all playing roller hockey. They had a
team called the Rockets.

Joe loved to play roller hockey and he was
good at it. He played all the time. "Maybe they
will let me join the team," he thought. "Then I

can make some friends."

There was only one problem. Joe's good skates were broken. He had another pair, but they were the old steel kind. They were slow and not good for hockey.

Joe put them on anyway and picked up his hockey stick.

Then Joe skated across to the park. All the kids stopped when he came along.

"Hey, listen to those skates!" one of them said. "You can hear them coming from a mile away! In what junkyard did you find them?"

All the other kids laughed. Joe didn't know what to say.

Then a big kid skated up to him. "What is your name?" he asked.

"Joe," he said. "What is your name?"

"I'm Matt," the boy said. "When did you get those skates?"

"A long time ago," Joe answered.

"I believe it," said Matt. "I wish you had better skates." The kids laughed again.

"Why?" asked Joe.

"Because then you could play with us," Matt said.

"My skates don't matter," said Joe. "I am good and I can prove it."

"All right," said Matt. "We'll play a little game. We will see how good you are!"

Joe and Matt stood looking at one another.

"This is your chance," said Matt. "You can show us how good you are."

"You be the goalie, Steve," Matt told another boy. Steve skated out to stand in front of the goal.

The goal was two trash cans. A puck hit between the cans scored a goal.

"You skate with me, Norm," Matt told someone else.

Then Matt turned back to Joe. "All right," he said. "Now you try to score. Try to put the puck between the cans. Norm and I will play defense. Steve is the goalie. The three of us will try to stop you."

Joe took the puck. He brought it out to the center line. It was about 30 feet from the goal.

"Come on," said Matt with a smile. "We are waiting."

Joe started to skate right toward them. He moved the puck in front of him.

Norm came out to meet Joe head-on. Suddenly, Joe took off to the right side. He got past Norm and headed for the goal.

Now Matt came out to meet Joe. This time,

Joe faked a move to his left. For a moment, it fooled Matt. Joe moved quickly out to his right. Suddenly, he had a clear shot at the goal.

Joe raised his stick off the ground to shoot. One foot was in the air. Suddenly, Matt banged into him from behind. Joe's left foot shot out from under him. Joe swung his stick as he went down. The puck took off high and fast. It headed straight for the goal.

9

Chapter 3

The goalie tried to stop Joe's shot. He threw up his arm, and knocked it away with his glove. The puck bounced away from the goal.

Joe hit the ground hard. He got up quickly, and tried to get the puck back.

Matt got to it first. He knocked it back across the center line. The game was over, and Joe had not scored.

"Let's play another game," said Joe. "Next time ... "

Matt cut him off. "I've seen enough," he said. "It's too bad you can't stay on your feet."

"You hit me from behind!" said Joe.

Steve, the goalie, skated over to Joe. "Nice shot you made," he told Joe.

"Thanks," said Joe. "You made a good save."

"I think this kid is all right," said Steve. "I think we can use him on the team."

"I don't think so," said Matt.

"Why not?" asked Steve.

"Because he can't stay on his feet," said Matt. "It's his skates. They are too slow, and they don't hold the ground right."

"You hit me from behind," said Joe again.

"Maybe I did," said Matt. "But if you can't take it ... "

"I can take it," said Joe. "But I don't like cheap shots."

Matt took a step toward Joe. "Well, I don't like cheap skates!" he said. He made his hand into a fist.

Joe came toward Matt. Matt was bigger than he was. Joe didn't want to fight, but he was not going to run away.

"Hold it, you guys," said Steve. He moved between them.

"You stay out of this," said Matt.

Steve turned to Joe. "I think you had better get out of here," he said.

Joe and Matt stood staring at one another.
Steve kept between them.

"All right," said Joe. "I'll go."

Joe skated away. He was angry.

The next day, Joe was walking up the street.
He saw Steve coming along, but Joe walked

right past him. He did not look at Steve.

"Hey, wait up!" said Steve. "I want to talk to you!"

"What about?" asked Joe.

"I'm sorry about what happened yesterday," said Steve. "You didn't get a fair tryout."

"It's all right," Joe said. "I'm not angry at you. It's that clown, Matt. Why do you guys put up with him? It looks like you're all afraid of him."

"Matt is not really a bad guy," said Steve. "It's all a big act he puts on. He likes to think he calls all the shots."

"He doesn't want me on his team. That's for sure," said Joe.

"Listen," said Steve. "Can you get a pair of good skates?"

"I already have a pair of good skates," said Joe.

"Where are they?" asked Steve.

"They're broken," said Joe. "They're at the skate shop, but they should be fixed any day now."

"That's great," said Steve. "We're playing our first game tomorrow. Why don't you come to it?"

"What for?" asked Joe. "Just to stand around and watch?"

"Maybe you'll have your good skates," said Steve. "Maybe you can get to play in the game." Steve started to walk away.

"All right," Joe called after him. "I'll try to be there. Thanks a lot."

The next day, Joe went to the skate shop. He went to see if his skates were ready.

Chapter 5

Joe's skates weren't ready yet. The skate shop didn't have the missing part. The missing part was a tiny nut. It held a wheel in place. The skates were no good without it. The man told Joe he had to order it. It would take a few more days.

Joe went home. The game would start soon. He didn't know what to do. He didn't feel good about wearing his old skates. But he felt he had to show up. If he didn't, Steve would think he was afraid. He felt he had to prove himself.

Joe put on his old steel skates. He skated over to the park. Matt broke into a laugh when he saw him. "Hey, look who is here!" he called out. "It's Cheap Skates!"

Most of the other kids laughed.

"I came to play," said Joe.

"Get lost. We don't need you," said Matt.

"Stay around, Joe," Steve called out. "Maybe we can use you." Matt gave Steve a mean look.

Soon the game began. The Rockets were playing a team from Green Street. The Greens scored three quick goals and led 3–0.

At first, the Rockets couldn't put an attack together. Matt wasn't passing enough. Often, he just tried to bull his way through.

Finally, Matt and Norm began making some good shots. The Rockets tied it up 3–3.

Then the Greens scored two more goals. They went on top 5–3.

It was getting late. Soon it would be too dark to play. The game would be over. Joe felt like a fool. Matt wasn't going to let him play. Joe started to leave.

Then something happened.

Norm scored again for the Rockets, but he was hit hard as he made the shot. He went down and didn't get up.

Matt and Steve helped him to the side. Norm had a twisted ankle. He was not badly hurt, but he was out of the game.

Matt looked over to Joe. "OK, Joe," Matt said. "I guess you are in."

"He can use my skates," Norm called.

"Thanks," said Joe. He put Norm's skates on. They were a little big for him, but they felt good.

Matt took Joe to the side. "Stay out of my way out there," he said. "Don't mess me up."

"Don't worry about me," said Joe.

The teams went back into action. Joe was playing winger now. The Greens were leading 5-4. The Greens' center beat Matt in a face-off, and he passed it back to one of his men.

The Greens' man shot it off to one of their wingers. Joe could skate faster now on Norm's skates. He got there in time to poke it away. Quickly Joe got off a pass. It went to Dave Leone, the Rockets' other winger.

The Rockets drove across the center line.

Dave got off a pass to Matt. Matt took a slap shot. He fell as he made it. It was high and wide. It bounced off one of the trash cans.

The puck came down almost at Joe's feet. He hit it as hard as he could. It was headed for the goal's left corner.

Chapter 1

Joe's shot slipped in under the goalie's glove.
It was a score.

The other players crowded around Joe. They
were clapping him on the back and shoulders.
Now the score was tied 5–5.

"Way to go, Joe," said Steve.

"Nice going, Cheap Skates," called Norm from the side.

"Let's get some more," said Joe.

Matt was still on the ground. "Hey," he

yelled. "I lost a wheel! I can't find it!"

A wheel had flown off one of Matt's skates. Both teams started to look for it. Dave Leone found it. It was in a pile of leaves near the goal. "The nut is gone!" said Dave.

They looked through the pile of leaves again. "Forget it," said one of the Greens. "We won't find it."

Quickly Matt turned to Joe. "Hey, Joe," he said. "Give me your skates—the ones you're wearing."

"You can use my old skates," said Joe.

"Come off it," said Matt. "Maybe you think..."

"You heard me!" said Joe.

Matt gave Joe a long, hard look. Then he slowly turned and skated to the side. He put on Joe's old skates.

"Let's go!" one of the Greens yelled. "It's getting dark!"

Now the two teams would play sudden death. The first team to score would win.

Matt lost the next face-off. He started to skate backward, but he couldn't do it on Joe's skates. Right away, he fell down.

Now the middle of the Rockets' line was open. The Greens' center skated right through it. Suddenly he had a clear shot at the goal. He raised his stick to shoot.

Joe raced toward the goal.

Chapter 8

The Greens' shot came in low and hard. Quickly, Steve fell on it with his body. It didn't go in.

Matt was slow in getting to his feet. He looked shaken up.

"Time out!" yelled Joe.

29

He skated over to Matt. "Here. Put on my skates," Joe said. "I'll use the steel ones."

"I'll be all right," said Matt.

"No, you won't," said Joe. "We will lose the game. I know how to use those skates, and you don't."

"OK, thanks," said Matt. He and Joe changed skates.

Matt took the puck out. Suddenly, he put on a burst of speed. Two Greens drove at him from both sides. Matt pushed his way past them and kept going.

On his old skates, Joe couldn't keep up. He pulled in behind Matt to back him up.

Matt raised his stick to take a shot. A Greens' man stood waiting to block it. Behind him, stood the Greens' goalie. They were both looking for a high, hard shot.

But Matt didn't make it. Suddenly, he drop-passed the puck back to Joe. Then he drove ahead, blocking out the Greens' man.

Matt's move faked out the two defenders. Joe shot the puck low, and it went in. The Rockets won the game, 6–5.

Joe and Matt skated back to the side together.

"Nice shot, Cheap Skates," Matt said to Joe.

"Nice pass," Joe said to Matt. "But why didn't you make the shot yourself?"

"I owed you one," said Matt. "Anyway, you are new on the team. You need the work."

Steve skated by. "Joe," he said. "We have another game tomorrow."

"Don't worry," said Joe with a smile. "I'll be there!"